Little Red Riding Minnie

 Book Seven

Disney PRESS

New York

Adapted from *Little Red Riding Minnie*,
written by Laura Driscoll

Printed in China

First Edition
1 3 5 7 9 10 8 6 4 2

ISBN 978-1-4231-4896-8
T425-2382-5-11128

For more Disney Press fun,
visit www.disneybooks.com

ONCE UPON A TIME, there was a kindhearted girl who was loved by all who knew her. Her grandmother had made her a cape of red wool as a gift. The girl wore it so often that her family and friends began to call her Little Red Riding Minnie.

One day, Little Red Riding Minnie learned that her grandmother was sick with a bad cold. She decided to bake a batch of her famous oatmeal-chocolate-chip cookies. Those were sure to make her grandmother feel better!

After the cookies had cooled, Little Red Riding Minnie put them in a tin. Then she packed a bunch of superstrong menthol cough drops in another tin. She thought her grandmother could probably use some of those, too.

Little Red Riding Minnie put both tins into her basket and set out for her grandmother's house.

The route to her grandmother's house took Little Red Riding Minnie through the center of town—right down Main Street, which was a very busy shopping area.

Little Red Riding Minnie loved saying hello to the shopkeepers as she passed their stores. She was enjoying her walk very much.

Then, just as she passed the post office, who should jump out of an alley and block her path but Big Bad Pete!

"Hello, Red," he said with a smirk. "And where might you be headed with that big basket?"

Now, Big Bad Pete was known to everyone around town as a scoundrel. He was certainly the last person Little Red Riding Minnie would have wanted to meet on her way to her grandmother's house. But Little Red Riding Minnie tried to be polite to everyone, and that included Big Bad Pete!

"Well, if you must know," Little Red Riding Minnie replied, hugging her basket tightly, "I'm bringing some of my famous oatmeal-chocolate-chip cookies to my grandmother. She has a terrible cold. Now, if you'll excuse me . . ."

And with that, Little Red Riding Minnie hurried away.

As Big Bad Pete watched her go, his mouth began to water. Little Red Riding Minnie's oatmeal-chocolate-chip cookies *were* famous—famously delicious!

Big Bad Pete had to get his hands on those cookies, even if it meant tricking Little Red Riding Minnie.

So, while Little Red Riding Minnie continued along Main Street, stopping to window-shop here and talk to shopkeepers there, Big Bad Pete ducked down an alley, raced along the backstreets, and zipped through some side yards.

Big Bad Pete arrived at Little Red Riding Minnie's grandmother's house way ahead of Little Red Riding Minnie. He knew he had to come up with a plan.

As he hurried up the front walk, Big Bad Pete spotted the grandmother's wash hanging out to dry on the clothesline in the side yard.

"Hmmm . . ." he said as he came up with a crafty plan to get the cookies.

Big Bad Pete grabbed the grandmother's clean

clothing and hid behind the house. He would be ready for Little Red Riding Minnie when she arrived!

Minutes later, Little Red Riding Minnie skipped up the front walk toward her grandmother's front door. She was singing to herself and didn't notice anything unusual.

Before she could knock, Big Bad Pete jumped out from behind a bush. He was disguised in her grandmother's clothing!

"Oh, hello, Little Red Riding Minnie," Big Bad Pete squeaked, trying to sound like her grandmother. "Have you come to pay your grandmother a visit?"

"Why . . . uh . . . yes," Little Red Riding Minnie stammered. Grandmother's cold must be very bad, indeed, she thought. She looks awful, and I have never heard her sound so squeaky!

Little Red Riding Minnie looked more closely at her grandmother and started to notice some peculiar things. Something was definitely not right!

"Grandmother," Little Red Riding Minnie said, "what big ears you have!"

"All the better to hear you with, my dear," Big Bad Pete replied in his best grandmother voice.

"And what big eyes you have!" Little Red Riding Minnie exclaimed.

Big Bad Pete crept closer to her. "All the better to see you with, my dear," he squeaked.

"And what big
teeth you have!"
Little Red Riding
Minnie continued.

Big Bad Pete
moved even closer.
Now he was right
over her. "All the
better to eat your
famous oatmeal-

chocolate-chip cookies with, my dear!" he shouted.

And with that, Big Bad Pete snatched a tin out
of Little Red Riding Minnie's basket, threw off his
disguise, and began to laugh wickedly.

"*Ah-ha-ha-ha!* I tricked you! Now your cookies are all mine!"

As Little Red Riding Minnie looked on, Big Bad Pete pulled off the cover of the tin, threw his head back, and emptied the entire contents into his mouth.

Too bad for Big Bad Pete . . . it was the wrong tin.

It took only a few seconds before the superstrong
menthol cough drops began to work their magic.
Big Bad Pete's face turned bright pink and his eyes
got large. He ran down the front walk and away
from Little Red Riding Minnie. He needed to find
a drink of water!

Just then, Little Red Riding Minnie's real grandmother opened the door.

"Oh, hello, dear," she said as she dabbed at her nose with a handkerchief. "Is everything all right?"

"Oh, yes, Grandmother," Little Red Riding Minnie replied. "Everything is just fine."

So Little Red Riding Minnie had a pleasant visit with her grandmother, who greatly enjoyed the oatmeal-chocolate-chip cookies.

Little Red Riding Minnie left the recipe with her grandmother and walked home, stopping to say hello to some friends along the way.

Meanwhile, Big Bad Pete decided that Little Red Riding Minnie's cookies were not all they were cracked up to be. As he drank bucket after bucket of water, he vowed never to scare anyone for their famously delicious cookies ever again.